A MONSTER & Me BOOK

MONSTER NEEDS A COSTUME

T0364034

This Running Press® Miniature Edition™ has been adapted from
Monster Needs a Costume, published in 2013 by Mighty Media Kids, a
imprint of Mighty Media Press, a division of Mighty Media, Inc.

Printed in China

9 8 7 6 5 4 3 2 1
Digit on the right indicates the number of this printing
ISBN 978-0-7624-6152-3

Published by Running Press Book Publishers,
An Imprint of Perseus Books, LLC,
A Subsidiary of Hachette Book Group, Inc.
2300 Chestnut Street
Philadelphia, PA 19103-4371

Visit us on the web!
www.runningpress.com

Dedications

To Aidan and Abigail,
*the greatest monsters a
dad could ever have.*

And to Tracey,
*who night after night put up with,
"Tell me if this sounds ok."*

Monster needs a costume
for his *favorite*
time of year.

I said to Monster, "Do you know what kind you'd want to wear?"

An astronaut?

A fireman?

A giant
Bartlett
pear?

He shook his head,
"I want to be a cowboy from the West.

And rope
some desperados,
with a star upon my chest!"

He rushed to find his badge and boots
but needed more than that.

We made his costume perfect
with a twenty-gallon hat!

Monster was excited
so he wore it *every* day.

But then he changed hi
mind when he discovered the balle

"I know the cowboy outfit was
the costume that I chose.
But now I'll be a dancer
and be nimble on my toes!"

Monster put
a tutu on

and danc[e]
around t[he]
kitche[n]

Pirouette, plié,

tendu,

and back to
first position.

He kept on dancing, day and night,
until his feet were sore.

But then he didn't want to
be a dancer anymore.

Monster took
his tutu off
and placed
it in the
drawer.

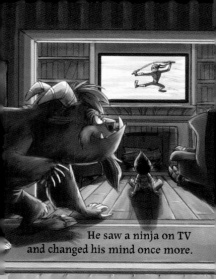

He saw a ninja on TV
and changed his mind once more.

"Now I'll be a ninja who is stealthy in the night!

Monster threw
a shuto

and some round kicks in the air.

And then he tried to vanish,
sliding underneath a chair.

Like a ninja he was quiet
and pretended to be small.
But spotting him was easy
since he's nearly nine feet tall.

Monster got discouraged,
and he turned into
a grouch.

He tossed the ninja costume,
    and he sunk into the couch.

He quickly put his costume on
  and gave a raucous roar.
  He hurtled down the steps,
    and then he bounded out the door.

From up the street and down the block
Monster was a sight!

The Dancing Cowboy Ninja
was the costume of the night!

AUL CZAJAK got an F with the
rds "get a tutor" on his college writing paper
d, after that, never thought he'd become a
iter. But after spending twenty years as a
emist, he knew his creativity could no longer
contained. He lives in New Jersey with his
fe and two little monsters. In addition to
e *Monster & Me*™ series, he's also the author
Seaver the Weaver.

ENDY GRIEB is a professional working
the Los Angeles animation industry and
ching animation. She is also an Annie
ward–winning storyboard artist, who has
rked as a developmental artist, illustrator,
d character designer for companies such
Disney, Nickelodeon, Sony, Klasky-Csupo,
ite Wolf, and more. She lives in Yorba
nda, California.

This book has been
bound using handcraft
methods and Smyth-sewn
to ensure durability.

The cover and interior were
illustrated by Wendy Grieb.

The text was written by
Paul Czajak.

The text was set in Olduvai,
Monod Brun, and
Wisdom Script.